THE **B⬤SS BABY**

DreamWorks

BACK IN BUSINESS

So, You Want to Be a Boss?

adapted by **Patty Michaels**

illustrated by **Patrick Spaziante**

Simon Spotlight

New York London Toronto Sydney New Delhi

SIMON SPOTLIGHT

An imprint of Simon & Schuster Children's Publishing Division
1230 Avenue of the Americas, New York, New York 10020
This Simon Spotlight paperback edition April 2020
DreamWorks The Boss Baby: Back in Business © 2020 DreamWorks
Animation LLC. All Rights Reserved. All rights reserved, including the right
of reproduction in whole or in part in any form. SIMON SPOTLIGHT and
colophon are registered trademarks of Simon & Schuster, Inc. For information
about special discounts for bulk purchases, please contact Simon & Schuster
Special Sales at 1-866-506-1949 or business@simonandschuster.com.
Manufactured in United States of America 0320 LAK
10 9 8 7 6 5 4 3 2 1
ISBN 978-1-5344-5776-8 (hc)
ISBN 978-1-5344-5775-1 (pbk)
ISBN 978-1-5344-5777-5 (eBook)

Table of Contents

Chapter 1

So, You Want to Be a Boss?

Hey! It's me, Boss Baby. You can call me Head Honcho or Numero Uno. Or if you're really short on time, you can call me BB. (If you're a boss, you're probably really short on time. I get it.)

I'm the Vice President, or VP, of the Field Operations Unit at Baby Corp. My field team and I are responsible for making sure that baby love is always at its highest level.

You may think that's easy, right? You'd be wrong.

Sure, babies are adorable and cuddly bundles of joy, but can you believe some people don't like us? Like Bootsy Calico,

who is trying to take over our baby world with evil kittens. Or Mr. Estes, a senior citizen who wants to steal all the love for elderly people.

Over the years I've learned not only how to be a boss, but also how to be a good one.

If you want to rise to the top just like me, you've come to the right place. With my wise business advice, you can become the boss of anything!

That is, anything except Baby Corp. That CEO chair is going to be mine.

Chapter 2

Negotiate, Negotiate, Negotiate

Let me begin by telling you something that happened recently at Baby Corp. To complete one of my field missions, I needed one of the best security systems in the baby business: the Gold Star Surveillance Package. It's a beautiful van that comes with state-of-the-art equipment.

5

There was just one problem. The CEO—
the boss of all bosses—rarely approved
requests for such fancy equipment.

I went into the office with Tim, my big
brother and the newest member of my field
team. It was time to teach him one of the
most important business skills: negotiation.

For those of you who don't know, negotiation is about reaching an agreement with someone by talking it out. If you're like me, it's a way to get whatever you want!

I gave Tim his very own copy of *Baby's First Book of Negotiation*. The book walks you through various negotiation tips, such as:

- Start with a compliment. My go-to line is, "My goodness, you are such a picture of good health." Everyone, including babies, likes compliments!

- Never meet the other person on their turf. That means that you shouldn't negotiate with someone in the place where they feel most powerful, like their own office.

- Remain cool and calm. Confidence is important!

- Ask for more than what you want. I started off by asking the CEO for the Platinum Supernova Surveillance Package. He eventually agreed to the lesser Gold Surveillance Package, thinking that he was giving me less than what I wanted. In reality, though, I got exactly what I wanted all along. See how that works?

Tim studied *Baby's First Book of Negotiation* like babies study their hands and feet. Then he tried out some of the tactics on our mom.

And guess what? Tim negotiated his way into eating ice cream with sprinkles at 10:30 in the morning . . . on top of a pizza!

Now that is some serious negotiating skills. I'm so proud of my big brother. He's really coming along in the business world.

Chapter 3

Step Up to the Business Plate

As a boss, I juggle a lot. Meetings, paperwork, phone calls . . . the list goes on and on. So when my parents surprised Tim and me with a vacation to Paris, I couldn't wait.

We boarded the airplane and buckled up. Then I noticed that Staci, one of the members of my field team, was on the same flight.

So was Jimbo, another field team member, and a lot of other babies. This seemed very suspicious to me.

Before I could find out what was going on, I fell asleep. Don't blame me! There's nothing stronger than the lure of a power nap.

As everyone knows, a long airplane ride is a baby's worst nightmare. (If you don't know, you've obviously never flown before.) Since I had checked out for nap time, it was up to Tim to protect baby love.

Tim had to think fast, because the babies were starting to cry. Loudly. Even worse, their bottles and pacifiers were nowhere to be found.

With Staci's urging, Tim snuck out of his seat and tried to sing the babies a lullaby: "Baby rides a shiny airplane on a . . . unicorn made out of hugs?"

Okay, so Tim might not be the best singer, but eventually it worked. One by one, he quieted the babies.

After a while, the babies started crying again. Local news reporter Marsha Krinkle was also on the plane, and she decided to film a report of the flight. The story would be called "The Crying Baby Apocalypse"!

If this story got out, baby love would fall to an all-time low. Babies would never be able to fly on a plane again, and they would definitely never get the respect they deserve.

The crying babies needed to be quieted immediately, but Tim wanted to lay low. The flight attendant had yelled at him for sneaking out of his seat earlier, and he didn't want to get in trouble again.

"I knew this would happen!" Staci cried. "You're giving up because you're not really committed. Do you even care about Baby Corp.?"

"You're right. I don't care about pie charts, or about who gets promoted," Tim replied. Then he thought for a moment. "But . . . I do care about helping my brother."

Staci's pep talk convinced Tim to step up to the business plate. He was going to do whatever it took to save baby love.

Swallowing his pride, Tim started to purposely trip all over the airplane. "Oomph! Ow!" he moaned.

As Tim tossed and tumbled, the babies stopped crying and started to giggle!

The happy babies were so adorable that Marsha Krinkle changed the news story to "The Giggling Baby Apocalypse"! Tim had saved the day.

I finally woke up when we landed in Paris. When Staci briefed me on what happened, I was so proud that my brother had proved his commitment to Baby Corp. It was time to celebrate . . . maybe with some milk bottles and a baguette?

Power Nap Time!

Anyone can nap, but only true bosses know how to power nap. Over the years, I've perfected the art of power napping into five easy steps.

1. **Set up your napping space.** Turn off the lights. Close the blinds, if you're lucky enough to have an office with a window. Most importantly, wear a bib so you don't accidentally drool on your best business suit.

2. **"Do not disturb."** Mute your phone and close the door. Don't let memos or company gossip get in the way of your nap!

3. **Wind down.** Close your eyes and relax. Think of something that makes you happy. Repeating the same sentence helps me clear my head: "I am the boss. I am the boss. I am the boss."

4. **ZZZ.** Sweet dreams of being a boss and achieving all your business goals!

5. **Wake up!** Power naps should be short. Make sure to set an alarm so you're not late to your next meeting.

Chapter 4

Think Outside the (Toy) Box

It was just another day at the office, or so I thought.

Suddenly, mysterious things started happening. I was taking extra naps. Jimbo was getting larger by the second. Staci's voice started changing too.

Then we noticed all our coworkers were

getting larger, and their voices were getting deeper. What was going on?

I quickly called an emergency meeting to brainstorm ideas.

When you need outside-the-box ideas, Tim is the best guy to ask. In fact, he insisted that his name wasn't Tim anymore. His name was space detective Dekker Moonboots!

That just goes to show you how many wild ideas he has.

Tim—I mean, Detective Moonboots—told us that we were all just having a growth spurt. Except at Baby Corp., growing up wasn't natural. Our special formula was supposed to keep us as babies forever!

To make things even worse, our CEO announced that every baby with a growth spurt would be fired. F-I-R-E-D!

In order to save our jobs, we needed to fix whatever was going wrong. We turned to Detective Moonboots again for his imaginative ideas. Maybe there was a bad batch of formula that had passed its expiration date?

"There must be a race of aliens that age backwards, from old folks to babies," Detective Moonboots declared. "They're trying to change the baby formula so they can be old forever!"

I knew I had asked for outside-the-box ideas. But this one was a little too far outside the box.

Then Detective Moonboots suggested that there were babies secretly living in the air vents of Baby Corp. Maybe these "vent babies" were messing with the formula and causing us to grow up.

This idea still seemed pretty wild, but we decided to investigate. And guess who we found? A real-life vent baby sneaking around our office!

The vent baby's name was Frankie. She wanted to be a true Baby Corp. employee and share her ideas with the company.

In order to stay young, Frankie had been stealing baby formula and replacing the bottles with vanilla milkshake. That's why the rest of Baby Corp. was aging—the milkshake had tainted the formula's effect.

Once we drank the uncontaminated formula, all the Baby Corp. employees turned back into babies again.

Phew. Detective Moonboots had successfully saved us from getting fired!

Speaking of firing, I wanted Frankie gone immediately. She was a threat to babies!

Detective Moonboots, however, thought that she would be an asset to the company. "Why don't you do something outside the box for once?" he said to me. "Take a chance on Frankie and her big ideas!"

I eventually gave in. After all, Tim—I mean, Detective Moonboots—worked hard and helped us solve the mystery, so I owed him one.

Who cares if Frankie is friends with her stapler? Sometimes a cubicle can be a lonely place. Imagine how lonely the vents are!

Chapter 5

Business Gets Personal

I was working from home one day when Grandma Gigi came down with a cold. We decided to call Tim's favorite babysitter, Marisol, to look after us. Then we found out that she was booked all summer: today, tomorrow, and forever!

But Marisol wasn't busy because she was

babysitting. She was senior sitting instead.

If this wasn't an attack on baby love, I didn't know what it was! Together, Tim and I devised a plan to make Marisol babysit again.

First, we visited Marisol. "I want to learn how to be a babysitter," Tim gushed to her. "I want to learn from the best! For as long as it takes!"

With his negotiation skills (and a lot more gushing), Tim convinced Marisol to take him on as a babysitter-in-training.

Together, they made a turkey and cheese sandwich in record time. "Some people call it time management," Tim bragged. "I call it Tim management."

Now, I always tell Tim that business is business. In other words: keep personal feelings out of work. At this point, I was beginning to worry that his feelings for Marisol were distracting him from our plan.

It was time for me to step in and put Tim back on track—the business track, that is.

I giggled, clapped my hands, and put on my best "adorable baby" show.

"Aww!" Marisol cooed. I giggled some more. Once she remembered how charming babies are, she would surely give up senior sitting!

But Tim became jealous of the attention Marisol was giving me. Business was definitely turning personal.

Tim and I got into a big fight, and it caused a lot of trouble. Let's

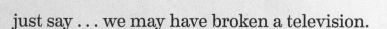

just say . . . we may have broken a television.

Luckily, before we destroyed anything else, we realized something. Tim had a big heart, and I had a brilliant business mind. If we combined feelings and business together, we could do anything.

Tim turned to Marisol, who has six little brothers. "I only have one brother, but I know there's nothing more fun than making him smile." He paused so I could give Marisol my best baby smile.

"You were born to sit babies," Tim continued. "It's more than just a business!"

Marisol melted. By tugging on her heartstrings, we convinced her to ditch senior sitting and watch babies instead.

Lesson learned? Sometimes business is personal too.

What's the Dress Code?

At Baby Corp., we dress for the job we want. That means something different for every baby. Let me show you some examples from my team:

My black suit and tie show that I'm not playing around. I mean business! At one point, I was convinced that *no* clothes made me a better boss. It turned out not to be true . . . but it felt pretty good to hear Tim scream every time he saw my naked butt!

Staci's ponytail and pink tutu look adorable. But her sweet look is actually a trap to make enemies underestimate her. Then she will take them down with no mercy!

Jimbo only wears diapers to work. It's the best way to show off that he is the "muscle" of our team. Have you ever seen a baby larger than Jimbo?

If you want to be a boss, it's time to start dressing like a boss!

41

Chapter 6

Trust in Teamwork

Change was in the air at Baby Corp. Our CEO had just been kicked out of the office. It's too long of a story to tell you why he left, but I'll just say that it wasn't pretty.

I was sure I was going to be the new CEO. But instead the company chose someone called Turtleneck Superstar CEO Baby.

I was disappointed, but I didn't let it get to me. Any successful career comes with a few setbacks.

After all, the selection made sense. The new CEO had helped discover a potion that would bring baby love to the highest level possible. The potion was called Stinkless Serum, and it erased all baby stink . . . even dirty diapers and sour milk!

Turtleneck Superstar CEO Baby asked me to keep the serum safe and hidden. "If word gets out about the serum, all our enemies will be coming after it," she warned.

The mission was so secret that I decided not to tell Tim about it. The less people who knew, the better. My lips were pacifier-sealed. Zip. Nada.

But then Tim found the bottle hidden under my pillow. He moved the serum to what he thought would be a better hiding spot: inside Grandma Gigi's giant purse! Tim thought he was helping me, but that was not a boss move.

I needed to get the serum back right away. Tim, thankfully, went out of his way to help me. He distracted Grandma Gigi with a very intense dinosaur dance routine while I dug through her purse.

It was an extremely tricky operation, but eventually I found the bottle of Stinkless Serum!

I learned something important that day: there are some people you can count on in your life. In this case, it was my big brother.

As Tim says, what's the point of being brothers if we can't trust each other?

I also learned to never hide anything under the pillow. (Except when you lose a

tooth. Tim told me about this lady called the Tooth Fairy who takes your tooth and leaves treats under your pillow. It's too bad that I'm never going to lose my baby teeth!)

47

Chapter 7
Family Comes First

I've left the most important business lesson for last. One night, I was trying to come up with a plan to finally defeat Bootsy Calico when Mom and Dad came into my office—I mean, my room. They announced that tonight was going to be Family Fun Night!

Tim was so excited that he screamed.

I was not as happy. My parents had no idea about the important business I had to do. I couldn't afford to have fun until Bootsy was defeated!

Today wasn't Family Fun Night. It needed to be Baby Work Night.

But Tim really wanted our family to spend time together. After all, it was the grand opening of Mr. Pineapple's Café, the newest restaurant in town. And there's nothing my big brother likes to do more than eat. (Me? I drink bottles. What's the big deal about chewing food anyway?)

I promised Tim that I would put work away and enjoy Family Fun Night.

When we got to the restaurant, I was on my best behavior. Having a tantrum in public is terrible for the Baby Corp. brand. I was even starting to have a bit of fun.

Then my business instincts started sending warning signs. The menu was filled with cat puns. Mr. Pineapple was a cat. And the restaurant owner was . . . Bootsy!

This new restaurant was clearly designed to raise kitty love and destroy baby love along the way. I immediately contacted Jimbo and Staci.

But when Tim found out, he became so upset. "You lied to me!" he yelled. "Tonight is supposed to be about family. I thought a businessman is only as good as his word!"

I tried to argue back, but Tim just yelled louder. "Why do you have to ruin everything?"

Ouch.

I had to admit that Tim's performance review was accurate. For business, my "word" was gold-plated and top-rated. For family, though, I hadn't been doing such a good job sticking to my promises.

I took a deep breath. Work can't always wait . . . but that's why you have underlings to get things done for you. I knew Staci and Jimbo could handle Bootsy Calico and his evil restaurant without me.

Baby business was important, but there's nothing like family.

After going home, the whole family snuggled together and watched a movie. Tim forgave me, and I was happy to be home.

I may seem like the model of perfection, but even I make mistakes. Everyone does. What's more, a good boss learns from their mistakes. In this case, I learned to keep all my promises. I also learned the hard way that family comes first.

Why am I telling you this? So you never have to make the same mistakes I did!

Chapter 8

Words of Wisdom

So, what do you think? Being a boss sounds pretty cool, right?

Since you got to the end of the book, let me leave you with some words of wisdom.

Believe it or not, I happen to know the best boss to ever walk this planet. He can do everything: negotiate, trust his team members, and even think outside the box sometimes. He's really the best of the best.

This boss once said, "The secret to success is to get your work done and go home in time for family dinner." Never forget these wise words, and you can be the boss one day, too!

Who is this best boss ever, you ask?

That would be me, of course!